All day long I Origami

while I eat my cold salami.

Lunch Box Mail
and other poems

by

Jenny Whitehead

Henry Holt and Company
New York

BUS STOP

Dahlin', won't you sit with me, read some poems, and sip some tea?

I
like
to
sit
up
on
this
wall
and
then
pretend
that
I
am
tall.

For Pete...
thank
you

A Flower for Christy

Henry Holt and Company, LLC, *Publishers since 1866*
115 West 18th Street, New York, New York 10011

Henry Holt is a registered trademark
of Henry Holt and Company, LLC
Copyright © 2001 by Jenny Whitehead. All rights reserved.
Published in Canada by Fitzhenry & Whiteside Ltd.,
195 Allstate Parkway, Markham, Ontario L3R 4T8.

Library of Congress Cataloging-in-Publication Data
Whitehead, Jenny.
Lunch box mail and other poems /
written and illustrated by Jenny Whitehead.
Summary: Poems about school and other topics,
such as haircuts, food, and going to bed at night.
1. Children's poetry, American. [1. American poetry.] I. Title.
PS3573.H4815 L8 2001 811'.6—dc21 00-25964

ISBN 0-8050-6259-9 / First Edition—2001
Printed in the United States of America on acid-free paper. ∞
1 3 5 7 9 10 8 6 4 2
The artist used gouache and acrylics on Arches 90-pound hot-press paper.

CONTENTS

ig
dog,
lease
don't
ick my
head.
an't we
just
hake
hands
instead?
/

slurp!

Appeteasers

Winding Down

Training Wheels

Loop-over-pull-through

Now I've learned to tie my shoe.

The 1st Day of School

Brand-new crayons and

unchipped chalk.

Brand-new haircut,

spotless smock.

Brand-new rules—

"No running, please."

Brand-new pair of

nervous knees.

Brand-new faces,

unclogged glue.

Brand-new hamster,

shiny shoes.

Brand-new teacher,

classroom fun.

Brand-new school year's

just begun.

The 179th Day of School

Broken crayons and
mop-head hair.
Scuffed-up shoes and
squeaky chair.
Dried-up paste,
chewed, leaky pens.
Dusty chalkboard,
lifelong friends.
One inch taller,
bigger brain.
Well-worn books,
old grape-juice stain.
Paper airplanes,
classroom cheer.
School is done and
summer's here!

Mom, I'm coughing.
Mom, I'm sneezing.
Mom, my head feels hot.
But please don't call the doctor—
I don't want to get a shot.
I don't want to leave my p.j.'s
and my blankey and my bear,
just to sit and wait forever,
freezing in my underwear.

I don't like it when the doctor
checks my throat—it makes me "ack,"
or when the icy stethoscope
hops up my front and down my back.
He'll probably want to look
for some potatoes in my ear,
or up my nose for gooey gunk
that keeps my head from feeling clear.

Then the doctor always says,
"Now rest and sip some soup,"
and makes me swallow medicine
that tastes like purple goop.
But if he makes me better,
I can play, I must admit.
Okay, Mom, I'll go—
but I won't like it,
not one bit.

It's Bath Time!

Soakin'
Soapin'
Shampoo.
Swirled-up hairdo.
Bubble-bath beard.
Shaving cream smeared.
Race boat,
Submarine.
Splash
Float
Squeaky clean.
Pull the plug—
Glug.
Warm towel hug.
Snug.

I Loth My Tooth

I whithle when I talk.
I wear a funny grin.
My thmile's got a hole in it.
I'm drooling down my chin.

Thure, I have a dollar
the fairy left for me.
But what good ith a dollar
when I can't thalk normally?

It's Off to Kindergarten!

The 1st Morning

"My precious dear,
my sweetie pie,
I know it's hard
to say bye-bye,
but please let go
of Mommy's thigh.
You're just a little scared, I know . . ."
"MOMMY, I DON'T WANT TO GO!"

Afternoon

"Why, look who's had
a happy day.
Your smile's so bright—
so much to say.
See, everything turned
out okay.
Tomorrow you'll do great, I know . . ."
"Mommy, I can't WAIT to go!"

Next Morning 🕐

"Okay, angel,
my sweet pea.
Here's one more
bye-bye kiss from me.
Now, please let go
of Mommy's knee.
We'll both be fine today, I know . . ."
"MOMMY, I DON'T WANT TO GO!"

Afternoon 🕐

"It's hard to be so
brave and strong—
to be away
from home so long.
Soon you'll feel
like you belong.
It's easier each day, I know . . ."
"Mommy, tell me that BEFORE I go!"

A Morning 🕐
(all too soon)

"Come back and kiss
your Mommy, please!
Before you go,
just one more squeeze.
My babykins,
don't scrape your knees!
You're growing up too fast, I know . . ."
"Mom, I really have to go!"

11

Inky dinky, boy, you're stinky!

Baby Babble

So sorry if the odor
from my diaper may offend.
And the only thing I do is drool
and sit on my rear end.
But give me just a year to grow,
and I'll be your lifelong friend.

Taking the Plunge!

I've got water wings and goggles.
I've got goose bumps on my knees.
And my big toe's just informed me
if I jump I'll surely freeze.
But if I'm brave for just one second,
I can swim all afternoon.
So, watch me dash!
And make a SPLASH!
'Til I'm wrinkled like a prune.

Start Here

I can read the CHUNKY on the peanut butter jar.

I can read the STOP sign when we're driving in the car.

I can read Beware of BEAST stamped on the shipping crate.

But reading Abraham Lincoln is still a little hard.

I Can Read!

I can read that Grandpa sent the money in my card.

I can read the URGR8 across the license plate.

I understand the N-A-P word Mom spells in the air.

I can read Red Riding Hood in my favorite chair.

Do You Have the Time?

"Good morning, Mr. Dibble."
"Why, good morning, Mr. Schnagel.
Are you free at eight to join me
for a pumpernickel bagel?"

"Oh, thank you, but I'm full;
I had some buttered toast at seven.
But how about a cup of tea
at quarter 'til eleven?"

"That puts me in a pickle;
see, I have so much to do.
At ten, I weed my garden
after bingo—how 'bout you?"

"I'll need to soak my teeth a while;
I ate a sticky prune.
But then I'd be available
for chicken soup at noon."

"We'd have to rush at twelve o'clock;
I take my nap at one,
and a tea party I must attend
starts after school is done.
So, how about a game of chess
back here at four-fifteen?
Then dinner at the diner,
where the special's canned sardines."

"Sounds splendid, but tonight
I have some leftovers to eat.
And six o'clock I always clean my ears
and soak my feet."

"Well, I'll be snug in bed by eight,
and snug in bed I'll be,
'til we meet back here tomorrow—
shall we meet at eight for tea?"

15

First ✚ Aid

The Sneeze

Achoo.
Bless you.
Tissue?
Thank you.

The Scrape

Boo boo.
Boo hoo.
Kiss you—
Like new.

The Flu

Hot head.
Cool bed.
Books read.
Soup-fed.

In Full Swing!

A Bad Hair Day

I have a little problem
and I don't know what to do.
I used to have a head of curls
and now I have just two.

It all began this morning
in the bathroom on a whim.
I thought I'd be a "hairdresser"
and give myself a trim.

I really meant to just pretend
and snip, snip, snip the air.
I guess my safety scissors slipped
and clip, clip, clipped my hair.

Then, I tried to fix it
but my brush was hard to hold.
I couldn't reach the mirror
since I'm only five years old!

Today I'll have to wear a hat
so Mommy doesn't know.
I wonder just how long it takes
for curly hair to grow?

Ways to Hide a Bad Haircut

Play dress-up all day long.

Keep your eyebrows raised while your bangs grow in.

Wear a bathing cap all summer.

Wear a really big bow.

Sweep two curls into one for that "cute-as-a-button" look.

Practice good posture.

Hope for rain.

Take up bird-watching as a hobby.

Plant flower seeds (they grow faster than hair).

Stinkin' Fish Blues

How I wish for a fish
at the end of this hook;
just a simple fillet
I can catch and then cook.
For hours I've waited
for lunch to swim by
and flop in my pan
smeared with butter to fry.
How swell it would taste,
lightly seasoned with thyme
and sprinkled with breadcrumbs
to soak up the slime.
My worm's a bit bored,
and I'm bored a bit, too;
this waiting is hard
when there's nothing to do.
I talked to a frog,
squished the mud with my feet;
I climbed up a tree,
and still nothing to eat . . .

20

I skipped a few stones,
built a fort out of sticks;
I collected some bugs,
and still no fish to fix.
How long must I wait
for my dinner to bite?
I guess I'll go swimming
and then fly my kite.

The afternoon's gone—
what a waste of a day,
no fish to take home,
and my worm swam away.
Maybe tomorrow
I'll just stay home and play.

Turtles and Snails

Turtles and snails.
Turtles and snails.
What could be slower
than turtles and snails?

Waiting for birthdays,
and popcorn to pop.
Afternoons wishing
the raindrops would stop.

Watching the clock
go ticktock in time-out.
Taking small bites
of a cold brussels sprout.

A season of baseball
your team never wins.
School on the day
before summer begins.

Turtles and snails.
Turtles and snails.
What could be slower
than turtles and snails?

The Car Ride

Passing cows,
Passing sheep,
Passing time,
Fast asleep.
Passing trains,
Passing tracks,
Passing time,
Eating snacks.
Passing maps,
Passing "where?"
Passing whines—
"Aren't we there?"
Passing hills,
Passing wheat,
Passing signs,
Grandma's street!
Passing comb,
Passing brush,
Finally here . . .
Bathroom flush.
(whew!)
Hi, Grandma!

APPLES

Welcome

Mail

Grandma's Street

My Collection

Beads and bugs and rocks
and stamps and coins and bits of string,
pennies, baseball cards, and books—
I collect most anything.

Stickers, marbles, buttons, bears,
and toys that I can wind,
magnets, bottle caps, and clowns—
whatever I can find.

I put my treasures in a box
or line them on a shelf.
I love to count the many things
I've found all by myself.

My friends enjoy collecting, too,
so trading's lots of fun.
This for that
and that for this,
it's fair for everyone.

And when I think I've found it all
and have the best selection,
then I know it's time for me
to start a new collection.

The Puddle

Hello, puddle.
How are you?
There's something
that I have to do.
I have no choice,
I must jump in
and splish and splash
and kick and spin.
I know you're sitting
peaceful there,
without a ripple,
without a care.
But though I try,
I can't resist.
These rubber boots
of mine insist.
So, little puddle
that remains,
I'll see you next time
when it rains.

The Dance Recital

Tutu twirl,
and tip, tap, toe.
Ballerinas
row by row.

Dancing, prancing,
fancy feet.
Whirling, waving,
smiling sweet.

Piano tempo—
plink, plink, plink.
Ballet shoes
in pink, pink, pink.

Sea of sparkles,
crown of curls.
Bop on top
of giggling girls.

Camera click.
Flash!
Video hum—
Daddy's princess,
Mommy's plum.

Curtsy, bow.
Clap, clap.
Encore!
Tutus twirl
right out the door.

The Bug Hotel

Hello, front desk?
How do you do?
So sorry to be bothering you.
But on behalf of all your guests,
I need to make a few requests:
Our room is kind of stuffy,
we could use a little air—
would you be so kind and tap
a hole or two up there?
I hate to sound too picky
or make a bigger fuss,
but baloney disagrees
with vegetarians like us.
Could you serve, instead,
some fresh green grass for us to munch?
And may I have a roommate
who won't eat me up for lunch?
We do appreciate
that we can rest our tiny feet,
and have the time to chat with bugs
we often never meet.
But when the day is through
and it is time for us to roam,
could you kindly let us go
so we can find our way back home?

My View at the Zoo

I stand on
my tiptoes,
stretched tall
as can be,
but the view
at the zoo
never changes
for me—
animal knees
are all that I see,
pair after pair
looking strangely
at me.
Furry knees,
backward knees,
spotted knees,
knobby knees—
where is the rest
of the animal, please?

So, once in a while,
will you bend
on YOUR knee,
and look at the zoo
from the view
that I see?
Or maybe instead
of you down here
with me,
I can ride
on your shoulders
and see what you see!

29

Sidewalk Art

Purple fingers,
orange knees,
squiggles,
giggles,
green dust sneeze.
Drawing flowers,
drawing faces;
pitter-patter,
rain erases.
Concrete canvas,
clean and new;
you trace me,
then
I'll
trace
you.

APPETEASERS

Dump one can of thick
tomato paste into a pot.
Add tomato soup—two cans,
and heat it 'til it's hot.
Throw in yellow cheese slices
and heaps of cooked spaghetti.
Mix the gloppy noodle clump
until it's smooth and ready.

Daddy's Spaghetti

When the big hand's on 12,
and the little hand's on 2,
you think of me,
and I'll think of you.
Love, Dad

Sweetie,
I baked you cookies—
chocolate chip!—
a dozen just for you.
Eat as many as you can,
then give away a few!
Toodle-oo!
Love, Nana

Here's your BLT
I made with TLC!
XOXO,
Mom

If I could,
I'd come to school
and kiss ya.
I'd hug you tight
and tell how I miss ya.
But then your friends
might laugh a bit and tease ya!
So, I'll just wait 'til after school
to squeeze ya!
Love, Mom   XOXO

CACTUS

Henley's Lunch

MICHAEL

MILK

ANIMAL CRACKERS

Kristen

33

A Submarine Sandwich

If I were a fish,
squishy cheese
would be nice
on some soft,
soggy bread
with wet mustard
for spice.
I'd add some baloney,
sliced rubbery thin,
with limpy leaf lettuce
I'd wash with my fin.
How yummy some
gray chewy pickles
would be
on my submarine sandwich
down deep in the sea.
I'd eat it with
cold, clammy coleslaw
to munch—
say, care to swim over
and join me for lunch?

Ding -a- ling!

Stop and listen—
Hear that ring?
That ding-a-ling
Means just one thing!
It's getting louder,
Move those feet—
The ice-cream man
Is on our street!
Run inside,
There's little time,
To find three quarters
And a dime.
Check the sofa,
Check the drawer.
Now I need just
Ten cents more!
Dig real deep
In every pocket.
Grab the piggy bank—
Unlock it!
Count the pennies,
Count them fast—
Hooray! I have
Enough at last!
Down the steps
And out the door—
To the four-wheeled
Ice-cream store!
Drat! He's gone.
He crawled right by;
So long, my chocolate
Ice-cream pie.
Tomorrow I will
Try again.
So, ice-cream man,
I'll see you then!

ice cream

Carrots? No, Thank You!

Some vegetables are good to eat,
and some are just okay.
My favorite vegetable's the one
that's really fun to say—

> Rutabaga!
> Rutabaga!
> Rutabaga!

It's really kind of tasty,
whipped up hot like mashed potata.
But I always start to giggle
when I'm asked, "More rutabaga?"

> Rutabaga!
> Rutabaga!
> Rutabaga!

You may like another vegetable
that has a funny name.
Chickpeas, leeks, and parsnips
may tickle you the same.

But I think rutabaga
is the best veggie that grows.
It's the only one I know of
I can laugh right out my nose!

> Rutabaga!
> Rutabaga!
> Rutabaga!

More ruuutabaga?

hee
hee

yes!

ha
ha

The Children's Menu

Hot dogs,
French fries,
Spaghetti with meat.
The menu never changes
no matter where we eat.
Jell-O,
Green beans,
Hamburgers and peas.
My tummy's kind of bored
always choosing one of these.
Carrots,
Grilled cheese,
Baked beans, and franks.
Order what I always eat at
home?
NO, THANKS!
Tonight, I'll try the lobster,
wild rice, and shrimp cup.
But, psst, waiter,
don't forget
to bring the ketchup.

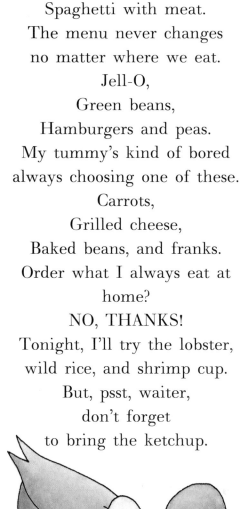

Supermarket Spies

Agent Bleach
to Agent Apple:
Do you read me?
Come in, please.
Are you staked out
by the steak?
Or under cover
by the cheese?
Captain M.O.M.
dropped off our orders
near the soup
in aisle 4.
Can you break
the secret code
so we know what
we're looking for?

Decode the Grocery List

1) T.P. 3-Ply x 12
2) 2 lbs. monkey treats
3) 1 can green wax
4) 1 carton uncracked chicken shells
5) 3 tearjerkers
6) 1 box of cartoon chow
7) 1 doz. icicles
8) 2 4-eyed spuds
9) 1 zoo-in-a-box
10) 2 oz. shredded moon particles

1) toilet paper
2) bananas
3) green beans
4) eggs
5) onions
6) cereal
7) Popsicles
8) potatoes
9) animal crackers
10) cheese

39

Bless This Food

Bless this food upon our plate
    that we're about to eat,
except, maybe, the casserole—
    it smells like Daddy's feet.
Bless the mixed-up corn and peas
    I lined up in a row,
and bless these things—
    what are these things?
    —in my yellow Jell-O.
Bless my dog who sits
    under the table by my knee;
if only he were waiting for
    some scraps of broccoli.
Bless, I guess, the orange mush
    my baby sister slurps.
Bless my handsome milk mustache
    and bless my little burps.
Bless my Dad so when he scrapes
    this plate he won't be cross,
to find the peas I'm hiding
    underneath my applesauce.
Bless the best cake ever baked
    in all the universe,
and bless my Mom for letting us
    eat dinner—dessert first.
    Amen.

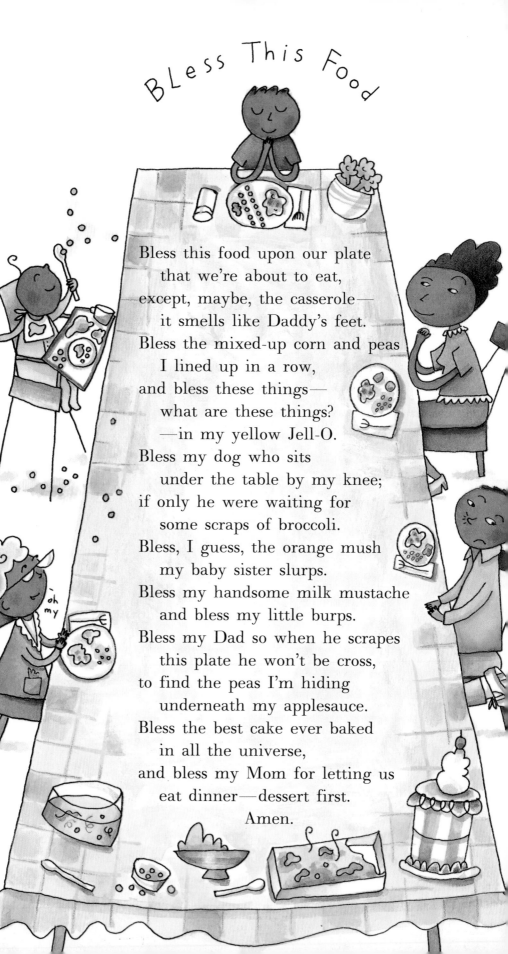

WINDING DOWN

Evening

A sherbet sky,
sun
setting
slow.
A porch swing
creaking
to
and
fro.
A mother singing
sweet
and
low.
A baby nodding—
off
he

goes.

Saturday Morning

I love to
go with Dad
down to
the corner
barbershop.
Not because,
if I am good,
I get a lollipop.
Not because
the chair spins fast
and cranks up
really high.
Not because
the trimmer buzzes
like a noisy fly.
Not because
I practice shaving
with the creamy foam.
Not because
the barber gives a
complimentary comb.
I love to
go with Dad
down to the corner
barbershop,
'cause nothing
could be better
than a haircut
with your pop!

My Kind of Flower

A grown-up garden's
lovely with its roses
all in bloom,
and lilacs
that remind me
of my grandma's
sweet perfume.
But I am
just as happy
with the flowers
that I find—
dandelions and clovers
I can pick
and no one minds.
I know they're
kind of droopy,
and they have no smell,
that's true.
But I can pick
a great big bunch
and bring them home
to you.

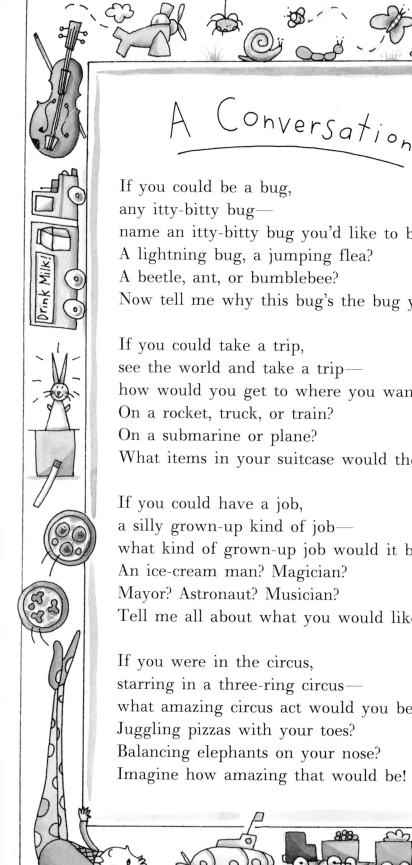

A Conversation

If you could be a bug,
any itty-bitty bug—
name an itty-bitty bug you'd like to be.
A lightning bug, a jumping flea?
A beetle, ant, or bumblebee?
Now tell me why this bug's the bug you'd be.

If you could take a trip,
see the world and take a trip—
how would you get to where you want to be?
On a rocket, truck, or train?
On a submarine or plane?
What items in your suitcase would there be?

If you could have a job,
a silly grown-up kind of job—
what kind of grown-up job would it be?
An ice-cream man? Magician?
Mayor? Astronaut? Musician?
Tell me all about what you would like to be.

If you were in the circus,
starring in a three-ring circus—
what amazing circus act would you be?
Juggling pizzas with your toes?
Balancing elephants on your nose?
Imagine how amazing that would be!

Make a Wish

A little bit of luck is always
waiting to be found—
a ladybug,
a four-leaf clover,
a penny on the ground.
Or if you'd rather make a wish,
no need to look too far—
Toss your penny in a fountain.
Blow an eyelash.
Find a star.
And if you made your wish
and wonder when it might come true,
it could be all your wish may need
is a little help from you.

8

Sweet Dreams

At
night
when
you're
tucked in
your bed and
can't sleep, and
you've said all your
prayers and counted
some sheep, look up at the
ceiling that's over your bed,
and watch pictures, like movies,
drift out of your head.
Imagine a whale racing boats in the sea,
and a big furry moose sipping make-believe tea.
Pretend there's a cowboy out riding the trail,
or a princess who sings like a sweet nightingale . . .

And, then, if you're
still not asleep you can try
to look out the window and gaze at the sky.
Fly into the night in a hot-air balloon,
and gather the stars on your way to the moon.
But if you return wide awake, will you stay
long enough to unwind and remember our day?
The ice cream we shared, the books that we read,
the bike ride, the park, and the ducks
that we fed . . .

And if you start closing your eyes,
feeling snug, think of me giving you
one last good-night hug.
And maybe, by then, all these
thoughts you hold dear
will fade into dreams
until morning is here.

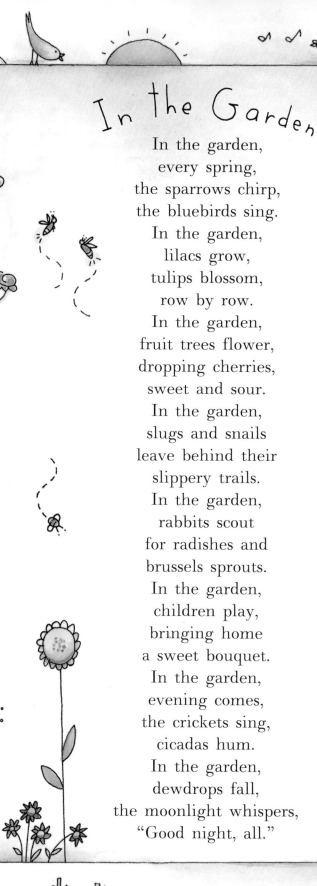

In the Garden

In the garden,
every spring,
the sparrows chirp,
the bluebirds sing.
In the garden,
lilacs grow,
tulips blossom,
row by row.
In the garden,
fruit trees flower,
dropping cherries,
sweet and sour.
In the garden,
slugs and snails
leave behind their
slippery trails.
In the garden,
rabbits scout
for radishes and
brussels sprouts.
In the garden,
children play,
bringing home
a sweet bouquet.
In the garden,
evening comes,
the crickets sing,
cicadas hum.
In the garden,
dewdrops fall,
the moonlight whispers,
"Good night, all."